# MAGIC BONE

## PUP ART

WITHDRAWN

GROSSET & DUNLAP
Penguin Young Readers Group
An Imprint of Penguin Random House LLC

The publisher does not have any control over and does not assume any responsibility
for author or third-party websites or their content.

*Library of Congress Cataloging-in-Publication Data is available.*

ISBN 978-0-448-48749-6                    10 9 8 7 6 5 4 3 2 1

# MAGIC BONE

## PUP ART

by Nancy Krulik
illustrated by Sebastien Braun

Grosset & Dunlap
An Imprint of Penguin Random House

For Danny, je t'aime—NK

A la mémoire de mon parrain Daniel,
et à Dorian et Timothy!—SB

# CHAPTER 1

"No! No! No!"

I bark as loud as I can. But my two-leg, Josh, is still pouring water all over me. And he won't stop. That's because Josh doesn't speak dog. And I don't speak two-leg.

So I'm stuck standing in this big dog bed. It's not a soft, fuzzy, comfy dog bed like the one I sleep in. This dog bed is hard and cold. And now it's *wet*.

I don't like hard, cold, and wet.

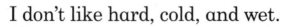

"No! No! No!" I bark again.

But Josh keeps pouring. *Splash, splash, splash.*

*Shakity, shake, shake!* Water flies everywhere!

Josh jumps out of the way. I guess he doesn't like being wet, either.

*Boing! Boing!* My paws are bouncing up and down. They want to jump out of this hard, cold dog bed. Here I go . . .

*Oomf!* "No! No! No!"

Josh is holding me down. And he's pouring more water on me.

*Splash! Splash!*

I'm all wet.

Now Josh is pouring something into his paws.

I stick my nose into

his paws and take a sniff.

*Sniffety, sniff, sniff.*

The stuff in Josh's paws smells sweet. Like a treat.

*Lickety, lick, yuck!*

That doesn't taste like a sweet treat. It tastes awful.

Josh starts rubbing the sweet-smelling, yucky-tasting stuff all over my fur. No! I don't want to smell like a sweet treat. I want to smell like a *dog*.

"Stop, Josh! Stop!" I bark.

I have to get out of here.

*Wiggle, waggle, whee!* My paws leap out of the cold, hard dog bed.

Josh tries to force me back in. But I push past him. I run through the house. Josh follows close behind.

I keep running. Fast. Faster. *Fastest.*

"Sparky!"

Josh yells my name. Then he says something else. I don't know what he is saying. But I can tell he is angry.

I do not like it when Josh is angry with me. I stop running. I look at him and cock my head to the side. That usually makes him smile.

But not today. Today, Josh is frowning and pointing at the floor.

I look down. I see wet paw prints. Josh must not like wet paw prints on his floor.

Josh reaches for me. I think he wants to put me back in the cold, hard, wet dog bed. I think he wants to slather gooey, sweet-smelling, awful-tasting stuff on me.

I love Josh. But I can't let him do that. I run through my doggie door and into the yard.

The yard is all muddy. Mud makes me happy.

I lie down on the ground and start to roll in the mud.

Now Josh is outside, too. But he is not happy. He is shouting.

"Don't shout, Josh," I bark. "Come and roll in the mud with me! It's fun!"

But Josh doesn't roll in the mud. He comes over and puts my collar on me. Then he stomps off through the gate. Now I can't see him anymore.

But I can hear him.

*Slam!* It sounds like Josh has just gotten into his big metal machine, the one with the four round paws. Now it sounds like the metal machine is going away.

Josh is gone.

And I am still here. All alone. With nothing but mud and dirt to play with.

But it's okay. I love mud and dirt. Mud is fun to roll in. And dirt is fun to dig in.

I run to where the flowers are. There's lots of great digging dirt there. I start to dig.

*Diggety, dig, dig.*

*Diggety, dig, dig.*

*Diggety, dig* . . . WOW! What's this? I found something buried deep in the dirt. It's a bone! A bright, sparkly, beautiful bone.

"Hello, bone!" I bark.

The bone doesn't answer. Bones can't bark.

*Sniffety, sniff, sniff.* The bone smells so meaty. I just have to take a bite.

*Chomp!*

*Wiggle, waggle, whew.* I feel dizzy—like my insides are spinning all around—but my outsides are standing still. Stars are twinkling in front of my eyes—even though it's daytime! All around me I smell food— fried chicken, salmon, roast beef. But there isn't any food in sight.

*Kaboom! Kaboom! Kaboom!*

# CHAPTER 2

The *kabooming* stops.

I look around. I see lots and lots of grass. And flowers. But they don't look like the flowers in my yard.

I don't see my tree. Or my fence. Or my house.

I don't know where I am, but I know where I'm *not*. I'm not in my yard anymore. I'm in some sort of park. How did I get here?

The meaty bone scratches against my teeth. Oh, that's right. My bone.

*That's* how I got here. My bone is

magic. This isn't the first time it has *kaboomed* me out of my yard and into someplace else.

The first time I took a bite of my magic bone, it took me all the way to London, England. London was fun— and *yummy, yum, yum.* You wouldn't believe the snacks the two-legs there leave on the floor for dogs like me. Sausages, cheese, fish, and *chips.* That's what the dogs in London call fries.

Another time, my magic bone *kaboomed* me to Washington, DC. I met my friend Fala there. He was a funny dog. He sneezed whenever he smelled flowers. Fala would sure have a tough time in this park! There are flowers everywhere!

I wonder where my magic bone has *kaboomed* me today. I've never seen a park like this before.

Maybe one of those poodles over there by the benches can tell me where I am.

At least I *think* those are poodles. They're attached to their two-legs by leashes. They have tails. And paws. And lots of curly fur, just like the poodles I met at my dog school.

But I've never seen *any* dog with fur that color. It's not brown or black or white or gray. Their fur is the color of the squishy salmon I ate in Tokyo.

I wonder if they speak dog. "Hi there, poodles," I bark to them.

They lift their snouts and turn away from me.

Maybe they don't understand me. Maybe they aren't dogs, after all.

"Did you hear something?" one poodle says to the other. She's talking dog! She's just not talking to me.

"I think it came from that stray over there," the other poodle says.

"I'm not a stray," I tell her. "I have a Josh at home."

But the poodles aren't listening to me.

"I don't talk to strays," the first poodle says.

"Strays are disgusting," the other one adds. She sniffs at the air. "He smells like a *dog*."

"Of course I smell like a dog," I bark. "I *am* a dog."

I walk over to the poodles and try to sniff their butts.

But they move away.

That's okay. I got a little sniff,

anyway. And I didn't like it. Those poodles smell like the gooey stuff Josh tried to rub all over my fur. Yuck.

The poodles and their two-legs walk away.

I never got to ask them the name of this place. Oh well. Maybe a nicer dog will come by soon.

But before I meet anyone else, I better hide my bone. I don't want any other dog to get his teeth on it. Because I will need my magic bone when I am ready to leave this place.

That's the great thing about my magic bone. It *kabooms* me to faraway places. But it always *kabooms* me back home again.

I think I'll bury my magic bone right here by these flowers.

*Diggety, dig, dig.* Dirt flies all around me. I want to bury my bone deep in the dirt.

I drop my bone in the hole, and *pushity, push, push* the dirt back over it. Now no one will be able to find my bone—except me, of course.

*"Bonjour."*

*Gulp.* Did I just hear some dog say *bone*?

# CHAPTER 3

*"BONE JOOR."*

I hear the words again. Louder this time. I don't know what a *joor* is, but I sure know the word *bone*!

I turn around to see a chubby French bulldog staring at me.

"Wh-wh-what bone?" I ask him nervously.

The French bulldog cocks his head. "Not *bone*," he says. "*Bonjour.* Hello."

I have no idea what he's talking

about. But I am glad he isn't asking about my bone.

"You're not from around here, are you?" he asks me.

I shake my head. "I don't even know where *here* is," I admit.

"This is Paris, France," the bulldog says. "Where are you from?"

"Josh's house," I answer.

"I never heard of that city," the bulldog says.

"It's not a city," I explain. "Josh is my two-leg."

"You have a two-leg?" The bulldog looks around. "Where is he?"

Um . . . I'm not sure what to say. I don't want to have to tell the bulldog about my magic bone that *kaboomed* me away from Josh's house.

"Josh . . . uh . . . went away in his metal machine with four round paws," I answer finally. It's the truth. Just not *all* of the truth. "Where's *your* two-leg?" I ask him.

The bulldog lowers his head. "I don't have one," he says quietly.

He sounds sad.

That makes *me* sad.

The bulldog shakes his head, hard. Like he's trying to shake the sad thoughts away. "Anyway, my name's Pierre," he says.

*Grumble, rumble.* Just then my tummy starts talking. And I know what it's saying. "I'm hungry," I tell Pierre.

Pierre laughs. "Hungry?" he says. "That's a funny name."

"My name's not Hungry," I tell him. "It's Sparky. But my tummy is hungry. Do you have any good scraps around here?"

Pierre smiles. "Are you kidding?" he asks me. "This is Paris. We have the best food in the whole world."

I don't know about that. I had amazing sausage in Rome. The barbecue scraps I ate at a Texas rodeo were incredible. And Josh makes yummy cheesy eggs.

"Come on," Pierre says. "I'll find you the best scraps you've ever had."

*Grumble, rumble.* My tummy sounds ready to give Paris food a try. So I follow Pierre out of the park. We walk down a long, narrow street.

*Sniffety, sniff, sniff.* My nose starts to twitch. It smells something *yummy, yum, yum.*

"What's that smell?" I ask Pierre.

"Crêpes," Pierre says.

I give him a funny look. "Crapes?" I repeat. "I've never tasted them. Are they like grapes?"

Pierre shakes his head. "No. They're thin pancakes filled with meat, cheese, or fruit."

I'm not sure what a pancake is. But I know all about meat, cheese, and fruit.

"Let's get some!" I shout. I start to run toward the smell.

"Right behind you," Pierre says.

The smell gets closer and closer as I run.

My paws run and run. And then they stop. Right in front of a big table.

I look up. There's a two-leg sitting in a chair. She's eating something. And in the chair next to her . . .

"Hey!" I shout to Pierre. "I know that poodle. She's mean."

Pierre nods. "Her name's Fifi. She thinks she's great because she goes to a groomer."

"What's a groomer?" I ask.

"A two-leg who cuts her fur and paints it that funny pink color," Pierre says. "He also gives her baths with flowery, sweet-smelling soap."

"Josh tried to put sweet-smelling goo on me," I tell Pierre. "But I wouldn't let him do it."

"Fifi's lucky," Pierre says with a frown. "She has a two-leg to feed her. She doesn't have to go searching for scraps."

"Do you want a two-leg?" I ask Pierre.

"It would be nice to find a two-leg," Pierre tells me. "One that needs my help. I would love to get up every morning and do something important."

I wonder what Pierre means by that. "I play with Josh," I tell him. "I sleep with Josh. And cuddle on the couch while he stares at that box with the teeny-tiny two-legs inside. Is that important?"

"Sure. If you and Josh think it is,"

Pierre says. "But what's important right now is getting some scraps." He looks up. "Fifi, how about tossing a little of that cheese crêpe down here?"

Fifi doesn't even look at us. She sticks her snout in the air. "I smell a stray," she barks.

Pierre looks at the ground. I can tell he feels bad about being called a stray.

"It's not Pierre's fault he doesn't have a two-leg," I bark back at the snooty poodle. "But it is *your* fault that you're mean!"

Fifi glares at me. Then she takes a big bite of food. She smiles as she chews it.

I really don't like that poodle.

"Come on, Sparky," Pierre says. "We're not getting any scraps from that dog. Let's go somewhere else."

I turn my back on Fifi and follow Pierre.

*Toot!* I hear a sound coming from underneath my tail. And I hear Fifi call out, "PU!"

But I don't care. I really don't like that dog. And neither does my rear.

Because that toot sure doesn't smell like flowers!

# CHAPTER 4

*Huff, puff. Huff, puff.*

My mouth is huffing and puffing. My tongue is sticking out of my mouth. I'm hot. And thirsty.

"Why are we walking up this big hill?" I ask Pierre.

"We're going to find scraps," Pierre explains.

"Can't we find scraps *down* the hill?" I wonder.

"We're going to a neighborhood where there are lots of two-legs wandering around," Pierre tells me.

"And wherever there are lots of two-legs . . ."

"There are lots of scraps," I finish. Two-legs are sloppy eaters. And they never want to eat food after it hits the floor. Which means more for me.

*Huff, puff. Huff, puff.* I walk a little faster. I can't wait to get to all those scraps.

I don't have to wait long. A nearby two-leg drops some sort of bread on the ground.

*Chomp!* It's chewy. And sweet.

"What kind of bread is this?" I ask Pierre.

Pierre takes a bite, too. "It's called a croissant. There's some raspberry jam on it."

I have never tasted anything like

this craw-sont. It is so *yummy, yum, yum*. But there isn't a lot of it. "I want more," I say.

"Follow the two-legs," Pierre says. "Someone else might drop one."

"How about one of them?" I point my snout toward some two-legs sitting in chairs.

"Those are the artists," Pierre tells me. "They don't eat. They just paint."

"They *what?*" I ask him.

"They put wet colors all over those pieces of cloth," Pierre explains. "And then other two-legs take the colored cloths home with them."

I will never understand two-legs. Why would they want to take colored cloths home with them? I would rather take food home with me.

There sure are a lot of two-legs standing around the artists' chairs. Well, around *most* of the artists' chairs, anyway. One of the artists is all by himself. He looks sad. I don't blame him. It's no fun to be alone.

*Wiggle, waggle, wait a minute.*

Maybe he doesn't have to be alone. Maybe he can have a friend. A *dog* friend!

"Do you think artists can use help putting wet colors on the cloths?" I ask Pierre.

Pierre shakes his head. "The artists don't like having dogs around."

That's silly. Everyone loves dogs. And even if Pierre couldn't help the artist with his colors, he could help the artist in another way. Having a dog around would make the artist smile. I bet he would have lots of two-leg friends around him if he looked happier.

Pierre is just scared. I will show him there's nothing to be scared of! I start to run over to the lonely artist.

"Sparky! No!" Pierre shouts after me.

But my paws are already running. Fast. Faster . . .

*Uh-oh!*

Now I hear shouting. Lots of shouting.

I don't know what the two-legs are saying, but I can tell they are angry.

Some artists leap up from their chairs. They wave their arms at me. I think they are trying to shoo me away.

Pierre was right. The artists don't like dogs around.

I don't like being around them, either. I start to run again. But this time, I am heading down the hill.

"Wait for me!" Pierre shouts.

The artists are shouting louder now.

My paws are really running. They don't like shouting any more than I do. Which is strange, because paws can't hear.

Those artists sure can move. But I am faster. Before I know it, I am at the bottom of the big hill—far from the shouting artists.

"I warned you," Pierre says as he reaches the bottom of the hill. "The artists only want to be around two-legs. I guess that's because the two-legs like their paintings."

I don't know what to say. I was really hoping Pierre and the lonely artist could be friends. Too bad things didn't work out that way.

*Grumble, rumble.*

And too bad we didn't get any more of that sweet bread. My tummy is still hungry.

"Can we get food anywhere else?" I ask Pierre.

Pierre smiles. "Of course," he tells me. "Let's go to the school."

School? That doesn't make any sense. I've been to school before. They teach you tricks there.

"I don't want to learn how to roll over or sit," I tell Pierre. "I already know how to do that. I also know how to hula."

"How to *what*?" Pierre asks me.

I stand on my hind legs. I wiggle my middle. "That's the hula. I learned to do that at a school in Hawaii."

Pierre shakes his head. "I don't know what kind of school you've been to. But this is a *cooking* school. You wouldn't believe the freshly cooked scraps you can find there!"

Freshly cooked scraps? That's *my* kind of school!

"What are we waiting for?" I tell Pierre. "Let's go!"

# CHAPTER 5

*Sniffety, sniff, sniff.*

Pierre leads me down a narrow street. It does not smell like yummy scraps back here. It smells like sour milk and rotten eggs. And I do not see any two-legs. All I see are big round metal cans with lids.

"These scraps smell awful," I tell him.

Pierre shakes his head. "The delicious scraps are in there," he says. He points to a small door that is propped open.

Pierre slips through the door. I
try to slip through, too. But it's not as
easy for me. I'm bigger than Pierre.
*Oomf.* It takes a lot of squeezing to
get me inside.

*Sniffety, sniff, sniff.*

I am glad I could fit through
that door. This place smells *wiggle,
waggle, wonderful*! Like the room in

my house where Josh makes the food, only better!

We only have one food-making room in our house. But the school has lots of them! And every one is filled with busy two-legs.

"What's that sme—"

"Shhh . . . ," Pierre warns me. "The two-legs are all in their kitchens now. But if they hear us, they're going to come out into the hallway and throw us out. Then we won't get any scraps."

I do not want that to happen. I shut my mouth tight so I can't talk. And I make my paws walk very, very softly.

Pierre walks past each room. He sniffs at the air.

I don't know what he's sniffing for.

But I think he's found it. He stops walking. His stubby tail wags back and forth. Pierre doesn't have a big tail, but it sure lets you know when it's happy.

"Aaah! Soufflé!" Pierre barks quietly, so only I can hear.

"Soo-flay?" I repeat. "What's that?"

"A really sweet treat," Pierre explains.

The smell of the soo-flay is drifting out into the hallway now. My paws start bouncing. My tail starts wagging. They are so excited. Which is strange, because paws and tails can't smell. And they can't eat.

But I sure can!

"Let's go get some soo-flay!" I shout to Pierre. My paws race in.

"Sparky, no!" Pierre says. "You can't just go in that kitchen . . ."

But I am already in. I run up to one of the two-legs.

"Can I have some soo-flay?" I bark to him.

The two-leg looks down at me and shouts. I don't know what he's saying, but I can tell it isn't yes.

A second two-leg starts to shout. I can't tell if he's angry with me or the other two-leg.

Pierre races to my side.

"You can't bark in the kitchen when they're making soufflés," Pierre whispers to me. "They need quiet to get all nice and fluffy in the oven."

"Then why are all these two-legs shouting?" I ask Pierre.

"I don't know," Pierre admits. "I don't understand a lot of things two-legs do."

I don't like shouting. I should leave. But I can't. I want some of that sweet soo-flay stuff! It smells so good! My tail thinks so, too. It's wagging wildly. Which is strange, because my tail can't smell.

*Bang! Crash!*

One of the two-legs leaps out of the way of my wagging tail. He slams into some bowls. The bowls fall to the ground.

Now all the two-legs are shouting. One of them opens a tiny door in the wall. It is getting very hot in here.

The sweet smell gets stronger.

*Wiggle, waggle, wow!* I think that two-leg is going to give me some sweet soo-flay to eat. I am so excited.

"Uh-oh . . ." Pierre doesn't sound excited.

"What's wrong?" I ask him.

"The soufflé fell because of all the noise," Pierre says. "They can't use it anymore."

*What fell?* I wonder. I don't see anything on the floor.

But something definitely did happen. The two-legs are waving their paws. And they are running toward us and shouting.

*Uh-oh!* My paws can't wait to get out of here. They start running fast. Faster. *Fastest.*

Pierre darts out the same door we used to come in. I follow him, squeezing myself back out. *Oomf!* We are back on that same small street. The one with all the big round cans.

I don't smell the sweet soo-flay anymore. I smell rotten eggs. And sour milk. Just like before. I like the smell of soo-flay better.

Just then, I hear two-leg paw steps heading our way.

"Someone's coming," I whisper to Pierre.

"Shhh . . . ," Pierre says. He runs and hides behind one of the cans.

I try to hide, too. But my tail sticks out from behind the can.

"You have to hide!" I tell my tail.

My tail tucks itself between my legs.

"Good tail!" I say.

I see a two-leg holding something in a bag. She opens the top of one of the cans. She drops the bag inside. Then she walks away.

"That was close," I whisper to Pierre.

Pierre doesn't answer. Instead, he knocks over the can.

Suddenly, I smell something sweet on the street.

"The soo-flay!" I shout. "It's in the bag."

Pierre smiles. "Two-legs don't eat soufflés when they fall. They only eat them when they are fluffy. I don't know why. They taste just as good." He paws at the bag until it opens. "Come on. Dig in!"

I walk over and take a big bite. The soo-flay is delicious! My tail starts wagging.

"I told you, we have the best food in the world here in Paris," Pierre tells me.

Suddenly, I hear paw steps again. There are two-legs coming this way.

"Maybe they are bringing us more!" I exclaim. My tail wags harder.

"They aren't bringing treats," Pierre says. "They're bringing trouble. They are *dogcatchers*!"

# CHAPTER 6

Dogcatchers! They have those in Paris, too?

I know they have dogcatchers in London, because one threw me in the pound!

And I know they have dogcatchers in Rome because one chased me through the Trevi Fountain.

Why do so many two-legs want to catch dogs?

"Run, Sparky! Run!" Pierre shouts.

"Come on paws!" I bark. "We have to run!"

Boy, can my paws move! Now I am running through the streets of Paris. I smell some yummy scraps, but I don't stop to look for them. I just keep running.

I am running so fast, my fur flies over my eyes. I can't see. But I keep moving. Fast. Faster. *F—*

*Boink!*

*Ouch!* I bump headfirst into a pole. That hurts!

"Stupid fur in my eyes!" I bark. I use my paw to push the fur away.

"Come on, Sparky," Pierre says. "Let's hurry past this group of two-legs. Then we can race up the stairs to the top of the Eiffel Tower."

Pierre points up with his snout. So I look up.

I see a tall building. At least I *think* it is a building. It doesn't have any windows. Just a lot of holes. And it doesn't have a roof. Just a point at the top. That point is up high. Way, *way* up high. It looks like it reaches all the way to the sky!

Yikes! "You want to go to the top of *th-that*?" I ask Pierre.

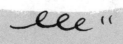

Pierre nods. "The dogcatchers will never think to look for us there. Dogcatchers only look on the streets for strays. At least that's what I've heard."

"But it's so high up," I tell him. "I went to the top of the Washington Monument once. It reaches into the sky, just like that tower. When I looked down from there, I felt sick. I don't want to get sick again."

"But . . . ," Pierre begins.

I do not wait to hear what Pierre is going to say next. There is no way I'm going to the top of that tower. So I start to run. I have to get away from this place.

"Sparky!" Pierre shouts at me. "You don't know your way around Paris. You can get in big trouble in this city. Wait for me!"

# CHAPTER 7

*Run, run, run.*

Pierre and I are zooming through the streets of Paris. The dogcatchers aren't going to catch us. No way!

I look ahead. No dogcatchers there.

I look behind. No dogcatchers.

I look down. No dogcatchers.

I look up.

*AAAAHHHH!*

Suddenly, my paws stop *zoomity, zoom, zooming*. That's because my eyes have spotted something really

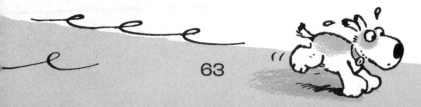

scary—*scarier than a dogcatcher*.

I wonder if this is the big trouble Pierre was talking about.

"What's wrong?" Pierre asks as he races to my side.

"Th-th-that thing," I say. I point my snout up toward a scary-looking two-leg. Or is it a bird? I can't tell. It has eyes and ears, a nose and a mouth. It is holding its face in its paws like two-legs do. But it has wings like a bird.

I've seen birds in my yard. They swoop down from the trees and catch worms in their beaks. Then they fly away.

What if that scary-winged, two-legged thing swoops down and grabs Pierre and me? I don't want to fly away!

I start to run again, so the scary-winged thing can't catch me.

But when I look up again, I see something even scarier. *"Aaaahhhh!"* I shout again. "What kind of four-leg is *that?*"

I use my snout to point to something that seems like some sort of strange dog. It looks like it has *three* ears— two on the sides of its head and a pointy one on top.

Pierre laughs.

"That's not a dog," he says. "It's a gargoyle. It's not real. It's made from stone."

Oh. That's different. I've seen stone things before, in Rome and in Tokyo.

"It's a statue?" I ask Pierre.

"Exactly," Pierre says. "There are gargoyles all around the building. The two-legs put them there to scare away evil spirits."

I don't know what spirits are, but I am sure they would be scared away by these creepy-looking gargoyles.

Pierre makes a face at me. "Do I look like a gargoyle?" he asks.

I laugh. Pierre looks silly. He's not scary at all.

I make a funny face. "I'm a

gargoyle, too," I tell Pierre.

Pierre laughs. "Good one," he says.

"If we pretend to be gargoyles, then maybe we can actually scare the dogcatchers away," I suggest.

Pierre looks around. "I don't think we are going to have to do that," he tells me. "It seems like we lost the dogcatchers when we made that turn a couple of blocks back."

That news makes me really happy. It makes my tail happy, too. It starts wagging really hard!

"So what would you like to do now?" Pierre asks me.

*Grumble, rumble.* My tummy answers for me.

"Can we find some more scraps?" I ask him.

While I wait for his answer, I lift my hind leg. A puddle of yellow water forms underneath me.

*"Oui, oui!"* Pierre answers.

"Everybody makes wee-wee," I say, repeating what Pierre said. I look down at the puddle of yellow water. "When a dog's got to go, a dog's got to go."

Pierre laughs. *"Oui* means 'yes' in French," he tells me. "I was just agreeing with you. We should look for more scraps."

*Wiggle, waggle, excellent!* "Let's go," I tell him. "All that running made me hungry."

"I think everything makes you hungry," Pierre laughs.

I don't answer. I let my tummy do the talking for me.

*Grumble. Rumble.*

# CHAPTER 8

"What's that German shepherd doing?" I ask Pierre as we search for scraps.

I point my snout toward a dog walking across the street with a two-leg. The two-leg is holding the shepherd's leash in one hand and a stick in the other.

"That's a Seeing Eye dog," Pierre explains. "The two-leg has eyes that don't work, so her dog sees for her. I sure wish I could find a two-leg who needed *my* help."

I feel bad for Pierre. He looks so sad. I wish I could help him, but I don't know how.

"I smell stray dog."

I know that voice. I turn around and see that mean, rotten poodle—the one with the funny-colored, flowery-smelling fur.

"Does Fifi do anything important for her two-leg?" I ask Pierre.

Pierre shakes his head. "All she does is act snooty and make fun of other dogs."

"Why don't you go jump in the river?" Fifi barks at us. "You could use a bath."

"Why are you always so mean, Fifi?" Pierre asks her.

"Sorry, I don't speak stray," Fifi

replies. "And your breath stinks. Did you fish spoiled sardines out of the trash? You strays are such garbage pickers!"

Pierre's back gets stiff. His lips move. I can see his sharp teeth. He is one mad dog!

"That does it!" Pierre barks angrily. "I have had it with that snobby poodle!"

*Whoosh!* Pierre takes off after Fifi.

Fifi glares at Pierre. And then she runs.

Fifi's two-leg is still holding on to her leash. But that doesn't stop Fifi. She keeps running, pulling her two-leg behind her. The two-leg is having trouble keeping up with Fifi. Four legs move a lot faster than two.

Fifi breaks free! She turns and starts up the same big hill Pierre and I climbed earlier.

"Fifi! Fifi!" her two-leg shouts after her. She shouts some other things, too, but I don't understand what she is saying.

Pierre is running right behind Fifi.

"Wait for me!" I shout. I race up the hill, right past Fifi's two-leg.

Two-legs leap out of the way as we run. Artists swoop up their cloths and bowls of colors.

Everyone is staring and pointing. I guess it isn't every day they see a two-leg running behind a sheepdog, who is chasing after a bulldog, who is trying to catch a poodle.

Fifi runs around a big puddle.

Pierre runs around the big puddle.

And I run around the big puddle.

Fifi darts between two artists.

Pierre darts between the two artists.

And I dart . . .

*Crash!*

Uh-oh.

# CHAPTER 9

Ooey-gooey colors are dripping everywhere.

*Drip. Drip. Drip.*

*Splash!*

Pierre steps right in a big puddle of ooey-gooey color!

That's when I see the lonely artist again. He's standing there, yelling— at Pierre and me. I guess those are *his* ooey-gooey colors on the ground.

"Ha-ha! You can't catch me!" Fifi shouts.

Pierre takes off after Fifi again.

His paws leave ooey-gooey colorful prints all over the artist's cloth.

"Wait for me, Pierre!" I call. I run after Pierre. *My* paws leave ooey-gooey colorful prints all over the artist's cloth, too.

I can hear the artist yelling as Pierre and I run off after Fifi. I do not know what he is saying, but he sounds angry. I do not think he is happy to have colorful paw prints on his cloth.

Josh did not like my wet paw prints on the floor of our house, either.

Why don't two-legs like paw prints?

Pierre stops running. He looks around. "Do you see Fifi?" he asks me.

I look around. I don't see the poodle anymore. "She must be hiding," I tell him.

"I'll sniff her out!" Pierre declares. "My snout is a super sniffer."

"My snout sniffs, too," I tell him. "Two super-sniffing snouts are better than one!"

As I look around for Fifi, I see the lonely artist. Only he's *not* lonely anymore. There are two-legs all around him.

I watch as the not-so-lonely artist gives the paw print–covered cloth to a two-leg. The two-leg gives the artist a pile of paper.

"I don't sniff Fifi anywhere," Pierre grumbles angrily.

Oh right. Fifi. I was so busy

watching the artist, I forgot all about her. "Maybe she . . ."

I don't get to finish my sentence. Because at just that minute, I spot the not-so-lonely artist. He's coming toward Pierre and me.

*Wiggle, waggle, what's happening?* The artist is running in our direction, like two-legs always do when they're angry. Only he's smiling, like two-legs do when they're happy.

How can anyone be angry and happy at the same time?

"Hey!" Pierre says suddenly. "Do you smell that?"

I stick my snout in the air. *Sniffety, sniff, sniff.*

I don't smell Fifi. But I smell something . . . *meaty*! Where is that meat smell coming from?

Pierre knows! He's walking right toward the not-so-lonely artist.

The artist is holding a piece of meat right in his paw. I think he wants to give it to us!

Pierre walks over to the not-so-lonely artist. He takes a big bite of the meat.

"Leave some for me!" I shout to Pierre.

The artist holds his paw out in my direction. Sure enough, there's some *yummy, yum, yum* meat in there.

I take a big step toward him and . . . *whoops!*

I just stepped in more ooey-gooey colors.

I bet the artist is going to be mad at me. Which means I won't get any meat.

"I'm sorry," I whimper, even though I know he doesn't speak dog. I look up at him and cock my head to the side. I am trying to make him smile.

Guess what? The artist smiles! And he gives me a piece of meat.

86

I look over at Pierre. He is splashing in the puddles of ooey-gooey colors and making paw prints all over a cloth.

"Pierre? Why are you doing that?" I ask him. "You're going to make the artist angry."

"I don't think so," Pierre answers. "The more paw prints I make, the more meat he gives me. Watch!"

Pierre dances on a piece of cloth. He leaves colored paw prints all over the place.

The artist gives him another piece of meat.

I want more meat, too! So I splash my paws into the ooey-gooey colors. Then I dance on a piece of cloth.

The artist holds out some meat.

*Chomp!* I grab it from his paw and gulp it down.

A group of two-legs has gathered around. They are watching Pierre and me as we step in ooey-gooey colors and eat meat.

I want more meat. So I step in the ooey-gooey colors again and make more paw prints.

The artist gives me another big hunk of meat.

Wow! I have trained the artist! I can get him to give me meat, any time I want. All I have to do is make paw prints on his cloths!

"This is fun!" Pierre barks.

"It sure is," I agree. "I love—"

Suddenly I hear something I do *not* love. The sound of Fifi's bark!

*"Hey! Little stray! You can't catch me!"*

That rotten poodle has come back to ruin all our fun!

90

# CHAPTER 10

"You have dirty paws!" Fifi barks at Pierre and me.

I don't get it. Fifi has a funny color all over her fur. Pierre and I only have colors on our paws. So why is she making fun of us?

"And you smell funny!" Fifi adds.

I don't get that, either. Pierre and I smell like dogs. She smells like flowers. Which is funny—for a dog, anyway.

"No wonder you're a stray, Pierre!" she barks, louder now. "What two-leg wants to be around a dog that smells like garbage? You'll never find a two-leg of your own!"

Pierre looks down at his colorful paws. His tail droops. Fifi has really hurt his feelings.

Fifi is the meanest dog I have ever met. I can't let her talk to my friend that way! Meat or no meat, I'm gonna get that dog!

My paws take off after Fifi! But the poodle is fast. She zooms between the two-legs on the street.

I'm fast, too. I'm right behind her!

Suddenly, Fifi's two-leg appears and snaps her leash onto her collar. She holds the leash tight and starts to drag the mean old poodle away.

Now that Fifi is gone, I can go back to getting more meat.

But when I get back to the artist, he's not holding any meat. He's holding Pierre! With a big smile, he lifts the French bulldog over his head. A group of two-legs clap their paws together.

They make a really loud noise. But it's not a scary noise. It's a happy noise.

Pierre is happy, too. His little tail is wagging wildly.

"Pierre!" I bark up to him. "Where are you going?"

"I found my two-leg!" Pierre barks back to me. "I'm going to be an artist's dog! I'm going to help him make art!"

The artist turns toward me. He starts to walk in my direction. He smiles and says something I do not understand.

"Come on, Sparky," Pierre says. "You can be an artist's dog, too."

The artist is smiling. He likes having a dog of his very own.

The two-legs who are holding

cloths are smiling. They like the paw prints.

Pierre is smiling, too. He likes making two-legs happy with art.

I am glad everyone is happy. But I do not think I would be happy being an artist's dog. I like being Josh's dog. Josh and I make each other happy— and that's *very* important.

I know someone who is *not* happy right now. Fifi! She is still being dragged through the crowd by her two-leg. Fifi's tail is not wagging.

"Pierre is not a stray anymore," I bark to her. "He's an artist's dog! And that's important! Much more important than walking around Paris being mean to other dogs, which is what you do all day!"

That makes Fifi mad. She growls. And shows me her teeth. She takes a step toward me.

Her two-leg tries to hold her back, but Fifi is one strong poodle. She leaps in my direction and . . . *splash*!

Fifi steps right in the middle of a giant puddle. She is a big, wet mess!

I walk close to her and stick my snout near her fur.

*Sniffety, sniff, sniff.*

Fifi doesn't smell like flowers anymore. Now she smells like wet dog!

"Ha-ha!"

"And just what do you think you're laughing at, *stray*?" Fifi growls at me.

"I'm not a stray!" I tell her. "I have a two-leg. His name is Josh."

"Oh yeah?" Fifi asks. She looks around. "So where is he?"

I don't know where Josh is. He went away in his metal machine with the four round paws. But I don't want to tell Fifi that.

Anyway, I know where he will

be soon. He will be home. And I want to be there when he gets there.

*Wiggle, waggle, time to go!*

# CHAPTER 11

I race back to the flower garden where I buried my bone. I start digging. *Diggety, dig, dig. Diggety, dig . . .*

There it is! My bone. My beautiful, meaty, magic bone. It's right there. Just waiting to take me home.

But wait a minute. What's that over there by the park bench?

It's a piece of cloth. Not like an artist's cloth. It doesn't look like something to dance on. It looks like something to chew on.

I pick up my new chew toy. Then I walk back and get ready to take a big bite of my bone.

But I can't bite my bone with a chew toy in my mouth.

*Thinkety, think, think!*

I know what to do! I dangle the chew toy from my snout. Then I pick up my magic bone with my teeth.

*Chomp!*

*Wiggle, waggle, whew.* I feel dizzy—like my insides are spinning all around—but my outsides are standing still. Stars are twinkling in front of my eyes—even though it's daytime! All around me I smell food— fried chicken, salmon, roast beef. But there isn't any food in sight.

*Kaboom! Kaboom! Kaboom!*

The *kabooming* stops.

I look around. There's my tree. And my fence. And my flowers. I'm back in my own yard! It feels so good to be home!

But I might want to go away again. So I better bury my bone to keep it safe. I don't want Frankie or Samson, the dogs that live on the other sides of my fence, to find it. And I don't want that mean old neighborhood cat, Queenie, to get her paws on it, either.

I run over to the flowers and start to *diggety, dig, dig.* Dirt flies all over the place. I keep digging until I have the biggest hole ever.

I drop my bone in the hole. Then I *pushity, push, push* all that dirt right back over it. My bone is safe.

Just then, I hear a noise. It sounds like Josh's metal machine with the four round paws. Josh is home! *Wiggle, waggle, yippee!*

I grab my new cloth chew toy in my mouth. I run into the house and hurry toward the front door.

Then I look down. My paws are covered in ooey-gooey colors.

Quickly, I race up the stairs. I jump into the hard, cold dog bed. The one that gets wet. And I wait for Josh.

"Sparky!" I hear Josh call my name.

"I'm up here, Josh!" I bark back.

Josh doesn't speak dog, but I guess

he figured out where I am, because I hear his paws on the stairs.

*Thump, bump. Thump, bump.*

"Sparky!" Josh says.

"Josh!" I bark back. My tail wags. Josh smiles. Then he looks down at my paws. And he gives me a funny look.

I wish I could tell Josh how my paws got ooey-gooey colors all over them. I wish I could tell him about Pierre. And the sweet soo-flay. And the scary stone gargoyles.

But I can't. Because I don't speak two-leg. And Josh doesn't speak dog.

Josh fills a big bucket with water. He starts to pour it all over me. But this time I do not run away. I know I have to get my paws clean. Josh does

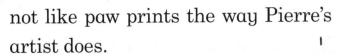

not like paw prints the way Pierre's
artist does.

Suddenly, Josh stops pouring.
He looks at the floor. Then
he bends down and
picks up my new cloth
chew toy. He gives me
another funny look.
And then . . .

*He puts my chew toy
on top of his head.*

"No, Josh," I bark. "A chew toy goes in your mouth. Not on your head."

But Josh doesn't know what I am saying. So he just stands there. With a chew toy on his head.

My two-leg sure is weird. But I love him, anyway!

# Fun Facts
## about Sparky's
## Adventures
## in Paris

# Tuileries Gardens

This beautiful public park was created in 1564. Originally, it was a garden for the royal family of France to enjoy when they stayed at the Tuileries Palace. But today the gardens are free to be enjoyed by everyone. And there is a lot to enjoy! In addition to trees, lawns, and flowers, the Tuileries Gardens are home to some of the most famous statues in the world. There are also lakes for boating, playgrounds, restaurants, and a carousel.

*The trees are shaped like boxes!*

# Montmartre

This busy neighborhood sits on top of a 427-foot hill in northern Paris. It is home to many artists who set up their easels along the streets. Some of them are there to paint the church or shops. Other artists spend their days painting portraits of the many tourists who visit the neighborhood.

# Le Cordon Bleu

This cooking school opened in Paris back in 1895, and is well known as one of the best cooking schools in the world. *Le Cordon Bleu* means "the blue ribbon" in French. Since the school began, people have come from all over the world to study cooking at the Le Cordon Bleu. In fact, the school became so famous that today there are thirty Le Cordon Bleu cooking schools located all over the world, including in Australia, Canada, Japan, Korea, Peru, Spain, Thailand, and the United States. But Le Cordon Bleu in Paris is still the best known.

# The Eiffel Tower

This giant iron tower was built in 1889 to welcome people to the World's Fair in Paris. It stands 1,063 feet tall and weighs about 10,000 tons! The tower is officially named for Gustave Eiffel, whose company built the tower, but many French people have given it the nickname the "Iron Lady." The Eiffel Tower is one of the most popular tourist attractions in the world. More than 250 million people have visited the tower since it was built.

1,063 feet!

# Notre-Dame Cathedral

Construction on this famous church began over 850 years ago and took almost 200 years to finish! The cathedral is mostly made of stone, but more than 1,300 trees were cut down to provide the wood needed to finish the construction. This earned Notre-Dame the nickname "the forest." The gargoyles that surround Notre-Dame Cathedral may be scary-looking, but they are actually very helpful. The gargoyles are really just fancy water spouts. They were built to move rainwater away from the roof and the sides of the building, to keep the cathedral from being damaged during rainstorms.

# About the Author

Nancy Krulik is the author of more than 200 books for children and young adults, including three *New York Times* Best Sellers. She is best known for being the author and creator of several successful book series for children, including Katie Kazoo, Switcheroo; How I Survived Middle School; and George Brown, Class Clown. Nancy lives in Manhattan with her husband, composer Daniel Burwasser, and her crazy beagle mix, Josie, who manages to drag her along on many exciting adventures without ever leaving Central Park.

# About the Illustrator

You could fill a whole attic with Seb's drawings! His collection includes some very early pieces made when he was four—there is even a series of drawings he did at the movies in the dark! When he isn't doodling, he likes to make toys and sculptures, as well as bows and arrows for his two boys, Oscar and Leo, and their numerous friends. Seb is French and lives in England.

His website is www.sebastienbraun.com.